Where Is the Queen?

Written by Marilyn Minkoff
Illustrated by Liz Callen

The Queen was giving a ball.

First, she set the table for eating in the
green room.

After that, she picked the songs for
dancing in the white room.

She worked hard all day long.

Then it was time for the ball to begin.

The King looked for the Queen.

Where could she be?

He walked into the green room.

But the Queen wasn't eating at the table.

Then he walked into the white room.

But the Queen wasn't dancing.

After that, he walked into the blue room.

He saw the Queen's table. He saw the
Queen's chair. He saw the Queen's
bed. Then he saw the Queen.

Sleeping!